A MOUSE IN THE CITY

In New York City, U.S.A.

You will never get away, Otis Mouse!

That is what you think.

I can hide in the museum.

This was not a good idea.

Otis jumps on the subway train.

That was a close call!

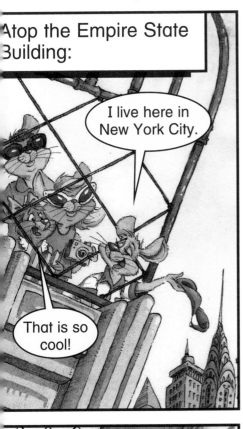

Atop the Empire State Building:

I live here in New York City.

That is so cool!

Otis sees the cat—again!

Where is that mouse?

Now I'm safe.

Free at last... I hope.

Otis is hungry and tired.

The taxi takes Otis downtown.

Otis loves to eat.

Later in Central Park.

He goes in through an open window!

I made it!

The cat is too big!

BAM!

That was close!

I will find a way in.

I have to hide.

I can rest in here.

Soon Otis is fast asleep.

The shoe gets packed in a suitcase.

The suitcase is put into a taxi …

Please take me to the airport.

… and then onto a plane.

Last call for flight 339.

When Otis wakes up...

Otis is in Egypt.

FAR FROM HOME

Otis wants to go back to New York.

I can hide in the shoe until its owner goes home.

Oh, no! He left! I have to find the man with the brown shoes!

I bet he went sightseeing.

Otis follows the man to the Sphinx ...

... and then to the pyramids.

The pictures on the wall help Otis.

Otis tries to free Nuru.

You did not forget me.

Never.

Whoa!

Nuru is free!

Let's get out of here.

Otis and Nuru run back to the café.

The man with the brown shoe is gone.

How will I get back to New York?

I can help you get back to New York.

OTIS ON THE GO

At the bazaar:

Here we are.

A snake! Get me out of here!

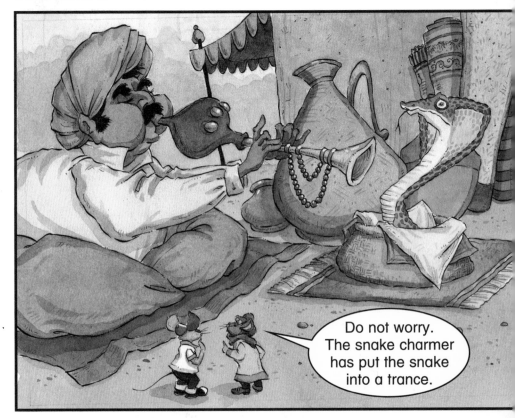

Do not worry. The snake charmer has put the snake into a trance.

At lunch:

Look, it is that nice snake.

He is not in a trance anymore!

Yum! Mice for lunch!

Hide behind the crates!

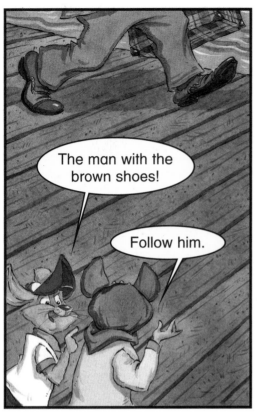

The man with the brown shoes!

Follow him.

That must be his ship.

You mean *my* ship.

HONK!

Bye, Otis. I'll miss you.

I'll miss you, too. Thanks for everything.

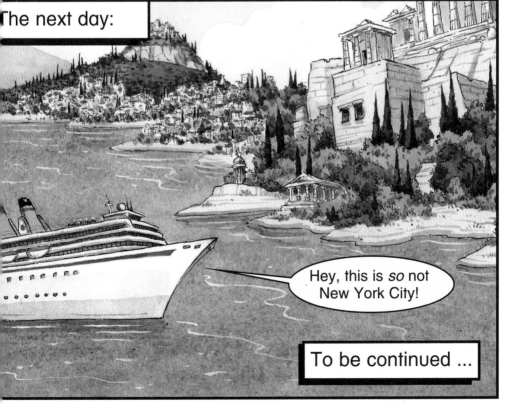

The Nile is the longest river in the world. It is about 4,130 miles (6,650 km), which is twice the width of the United States.

Cairo

Egypt

Luxor

The Egyptian pyramids were royal tombs. The kings and queens of ancient Egypt were buried in them.

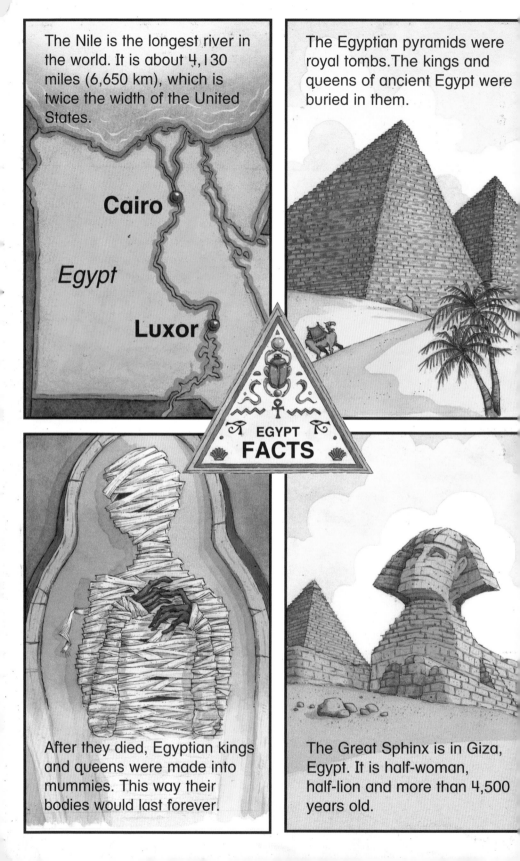

EGYPT **FACTS**

After they died, Egyptian kings and queens were made into mummies. This way their bodies would last forever.

The Great Sphinx is in Giza, Egypt. It is half-woman, half-lion and more than 4,500 years old.